Holly Keller

HELP!

A Story of
Friendship

Greenwillow Books
An Imprint of HarperCollins Publishers

Help! A Story of Friendship. Copyright © 2007 by Holly Keller. All rights reserved. Manufactured in China. www.harpercollinschildrens.com
Collographs and watercolors were used to prepare the full-color art. The text type is 22-point Clichee.

Library of Congress Cataloging-in Publication Data. Keller, Holly. Help! : a story of friendship / by Holly Keller. p. cm. "Greenwillow Books."
Summary: Mouse hears a rumor that snakes do not like mice and while trying to avoid his former friend, Snake,
he falls into a hole from which neither Hedgehog, Squirrel, nor Rabbit can help him out.
ISBN-13: 978-0-06-123913-7 (trade bdg.) ISBN-10: 0-06-123913-5 (trade bdg.)
ISBN-13: 978-0-06-123914-4 (lib. bdg.) ISBN-10: 0-06-123914-3 (lib. bdg.)
[1. Fear—Fiction. 2. Friendship—Fiction. 3. Animals—Fiction.] I. Title.
PZ7.K28132 Hdv 2007 [E]—dc 22 2006032116

First Edition 10 9 8 7 6 5 4 3 2
Greenwillow Books

To Barbara, Clarice, Deirdre, Gerry, Helene,

Jane, Judy, Kate, Liz, Mary, Oi, and Tung

for their forbearance

One morning Hedgehog found Mouse covering himself with leaves.

"What in the world are you doing?" asked Hedgehog.

"I'm hiding," said Mouse, "from Snake."

"From our *friend* Snake?" asked Hedgehog.

"Yes," Mouse whispered. "Fox told Skunk and Skunk told me that snakes are very dangerous to mice."

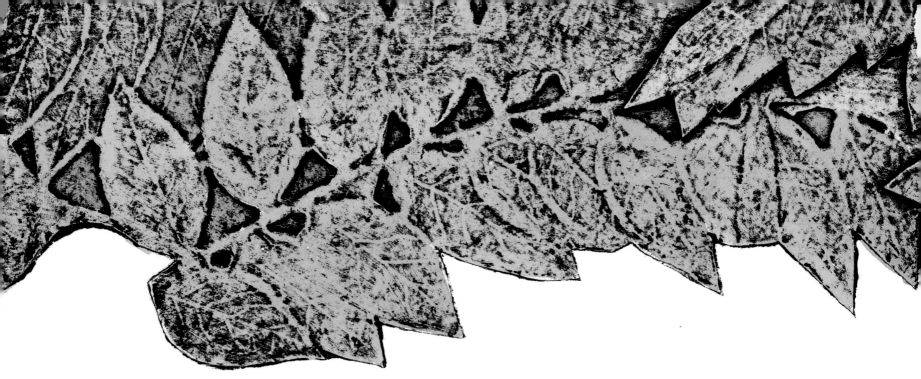

"That's silly gossip," said Hedgehog. "You know Snake would never hurt you. Come on. We can walk together, and you will be perfectly safe."

Mouse hesitated.

"I insist," said Hedgehog.

So Mouse went along.

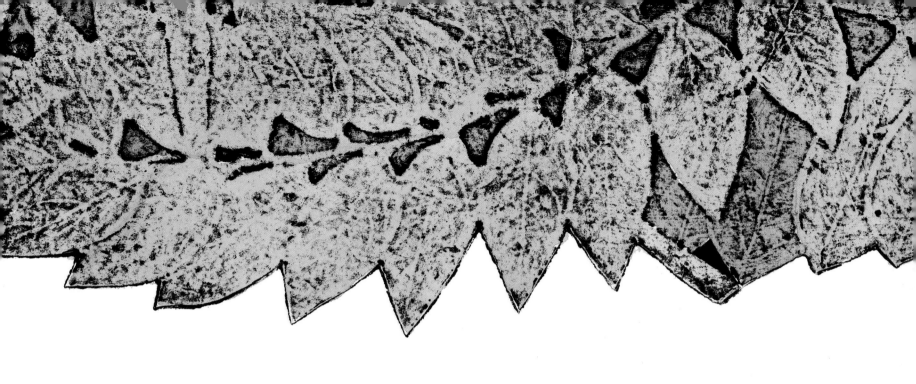

Hedgehog talked about little things, but Mouse wasn't paying attention. He was still worrying about Snake. He looked around nervously.

He looked everywhere but at his feet.

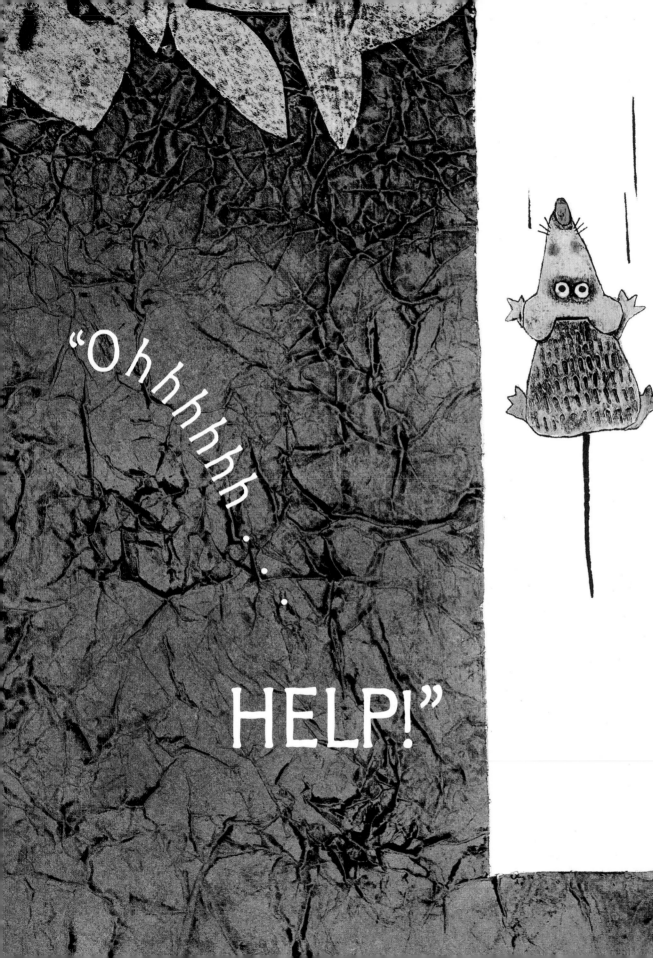

"Ohhhhhh . . . . HELP!"

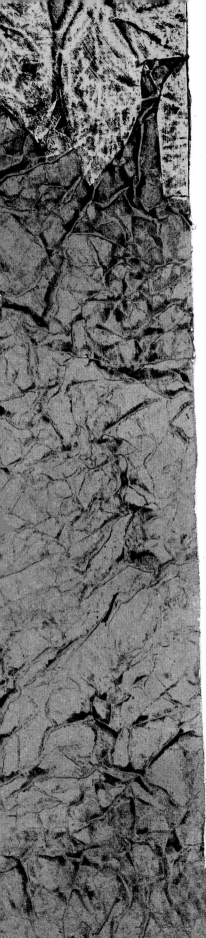

Hedgehog peered down.
"You should be afraid of
yourself, Mouse, not of Snake."

"It's not funny," Mouse yelled.
"I've hurt my foot and I can't get
out."

"Are you sure?" Hedgehog
shouted.

"Yes!" Mouse yelled.

"Stay calm," said Hedgehog.
"I'll get help."

Just then Squirrel walked by.

"Mouse has gotten it into his head to be afraid of Snake," said Hedgehog. "He was so nervous that he didn't watch where he was going. He fell into a hole and hurt his foot, and now he can't get out. Can you help?"

But Squirrel couldn't help.

"It will be too dark," she said, "and there might be spiders."

Rabbit came along, and Hedgehog told him about Mouse and Snake. "You know how to go down holes," said Hedgehog.

Rabbit looked into the hole. "Hello, Mouse!" he yelled.

"It's too deep," Rabbit said to Hedgehog, "and the walls are too straight. I wouldn't be able to hop out."

"Why don't *you* go, Hedgehog?" asked Squirrel.

"Because Mouse would have to get on my back, and my prickles would hurt him," Hedgehog said.

Mouse started to cry.

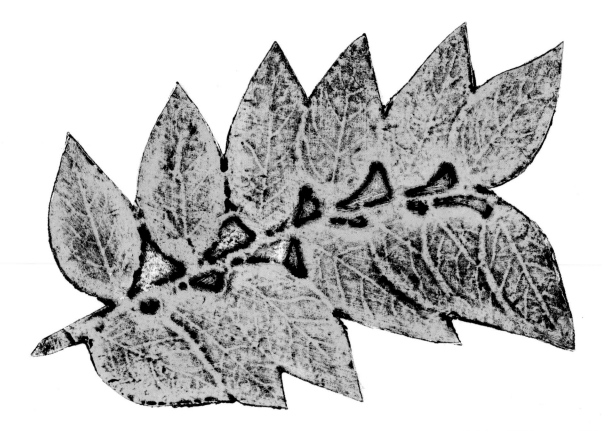

Wishywishywishy . . .

Hedgehog heard the grass move.

It was Snake.

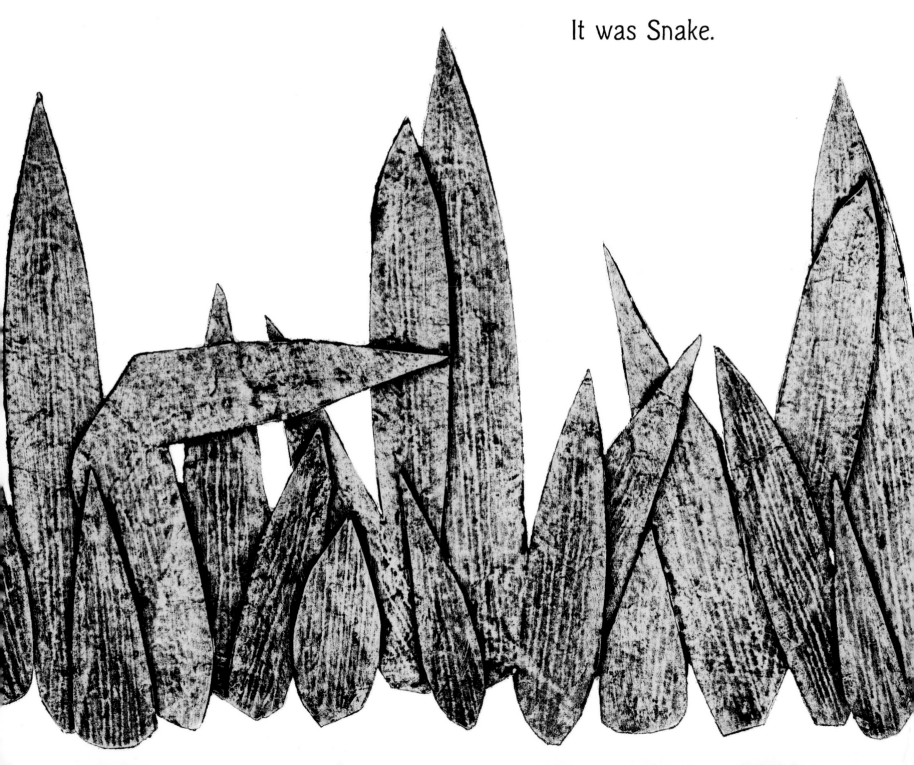

"What's going on?" said Snake.

"Shhhhh!" Hedgehog whispered. "Mouse fell into a deep, dark hole. He hurt his foot and he can't get out."

"Is it a secret?" Snake whispered back.

"Not exactly," whispered Hedgehog. "It's just that we don't know how to get him out. Squirrel is afraid to go down by herself, Rabbit wouldn't be able hop out, and I'm too prickly."

"Then I'll go down," Snake said. "No problem."

"Oh, no," said Hedgehog. "That's not a good idea at all."

"Not at all," said Squirrel.

"Not at all," said Rabbit.

"You see, Snake," Hedgehog said, "Fox told Skunk and Skunk told Mouse that snakes are dangerous to mice. Mouse was trying to hide from *you* when he fell into the hole."

"But I have always been Mouse's friend," said Snake.

"Of course you have," said Hedgehog.

"So I am going to rescue Mouse anyway," said Snake.

"How will you do it without scaring Mouse?" asked Hedgehog.

"Someone get a stick,"
said Snake.
Squirrel did it.

"Now tie my tail around it,"
said Snake.
Rabbit did it.

"Now make sure the
knot is tight."
Hedgehog did it.

"Now watch!"

When Mouse saw the stick,

he grabbed it.

Snake began to climb the tree,

and slowly Mouse came up.

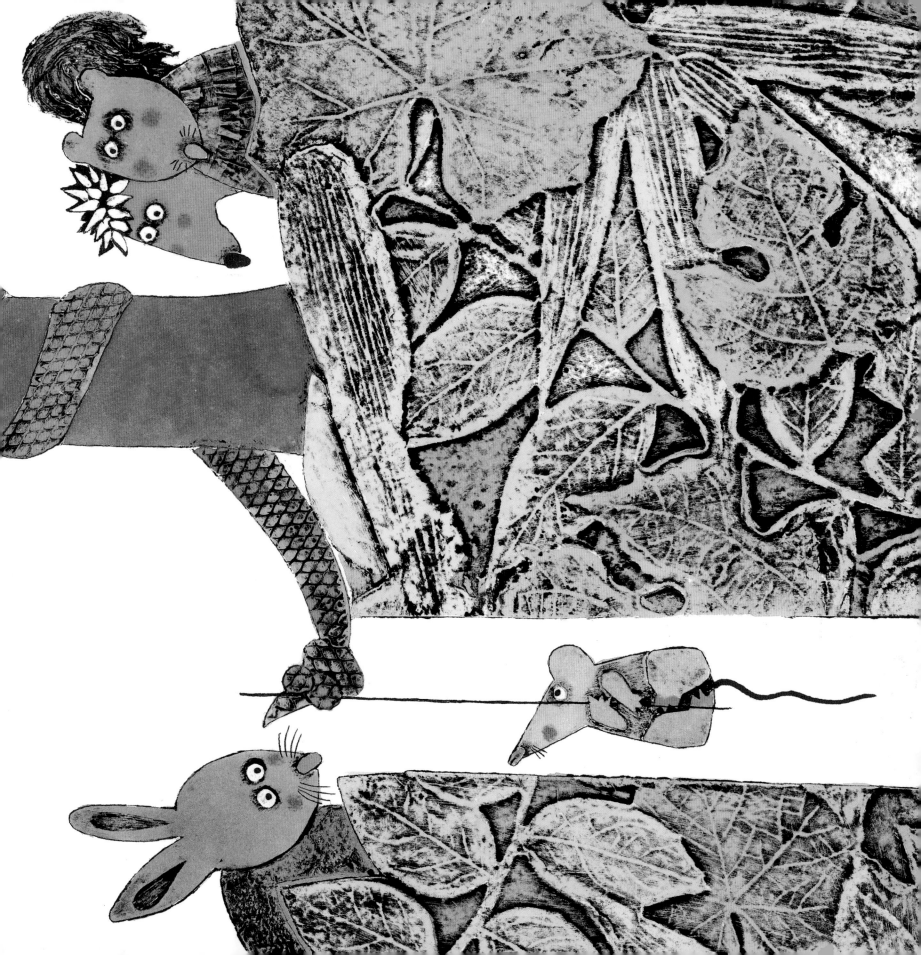

Mouse saw Snake and gasped.

Then he saw the stick still tied to Snake's tail.

"Snake saved you," said Hedgehog.

"He did," said Squirrel.

"He rescued you," said Rabbit.

"Because I would never hurt you," Snake said.

Mouse turned a deep shade of pink.

"I am very sorry," he said.

Snake, Squirrel, Hedgehog, and Rabbit helped Mouse hobble home.

They bandaged Mouse's foot, and he lay down to rest.

Several mornings later, Hedgehog was taking his walk, and along came Mouse. He was holding a bouquet of flowers.

"Where are you going?" asked Hedgehog.

"I'm going to say thank you to Snake," said Mouse, "and to give him some flowers that I picked."

And Snake was very pleased to have them.